JAZZI'S JOURNEY :

When I Grow Up What Will I Be?
A Doctor, A Teacher, Maybe An MC!

Enjoy the journey!
Dr. Margaret Starkes
2/2022

Written by
Dr. Margaret J. Starkes

Illustrated by
Michael Ragland

1

When I
Grow Up
What Will I Be?
A Doctor,
A Teacher,
Maybe An MC!

Acknowledgements by the author, Dr. Margaret J. Starkes

To the Creator of the sun, moon and the stars, my Father-I thank you for choosing to use me.

I am my Sister's Keeper - because of you, I am.
With love, John and MaryLou's baby #LousLegacy

This book is dedicated to children everywhere. Dare to believe in the beauty of your dreams.
You are filled with potential and purpose. Remember that no one can determine
your destiny but you! Make all of your dreams come true.

To my three reasons why, Isaiah, Nile and Zion-
I thank God for sending me you.

Jazzi's Journey: When I Grow Up, What Will I Be? A Doctor, A Teacher, Maybe An MC!

Text copyright © 2021 - Dr. Margaret J. Starkes

Cover art, book design and illustrations © 2021 - Michael Ragland

For permission requests, write to these email addresses:
Dr. Margaret J. Starkes: drmjstarkes@yahoo.com
Michael Ragland: mragland.art@gmail.com

Published by W.E. Publishing Company, LLC

ISBN-10: 8497544428
ISBN-13: 979-8497544428

Printed in the United States of America

Meet Jazzi. She loves reading, history, writing, double-dutch and rap music. She's got big dreams and she wants the whole world to know it! She is the youngest of six children and when her siblings grew up and moved out of the house, she and her parents decided to move into a townhouse apartment in a recently renovated city neighborhood.

Jazzi's dad is a custodian at her school. Her mom works from home and has a home-cooked meal waiting for her every single day! Everyone in the building loves the smell of her mama's cooking. Most days, she makes enough and shares it with anyone who comes by.

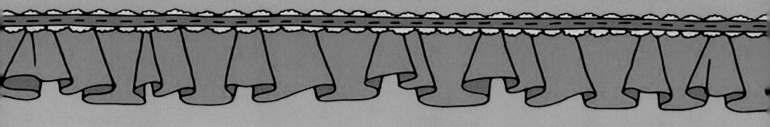

Jazzi and her mom are best friends. They dance together, cook together, and listen to music all the time, especially old school rap music! After all, her mom was a former rap artist in the city, so Jazzi grew up listening to 80's hip hop.

Some people call her an old soul because she loves female rap legends like Salt-n-Pepa, Queen Latifah and MC Lyte. Because of her mother's love of old school rap, Jazzi's been rhyming since she could speak.

Jazzi loves learning and going to school to spend time with her friends. She's an honor student at Lou's Legacy: Center for the Performing Arts, where she's been at the top of her class since day one. It's the last day of school before summer vacation and excitement fills the air as Jazzi and her mom walk to school for her last day as a fourth grade scholar.

It was a lovely day, and Jazzi and her mom were walking to school singing one of their favorite tunes when Jazzi's friends caught up with them.

"Good morning, girls."

"Hey Jazzi's mom, Hey Jazz," the girls reply in unison!

"We were just about to do our daily affirmations. Would you like to join us?"

"Yes ma'am."

"Okay, repeat after me."

"Today, I will be great. On time and never late. I'll do my best to achieve. In myself I will believe. My mind is alert and I'm all set to make this the best learning day yet."

She gives the girls a high five and they head off.

The girls enter the building and head to their favorite class with Sister Rose. Sister Rose is the most popular teacher at Lou's Legacy. Everyone loves her! She's smart, she's beautiful, and she sings like a bird.

As the students entered the class, Sister Rose asked everyone to meet in the Unity Circle for a class check in. "Good morning, Scholars. Let's continue talking about our life goals and plans for the future. Who would like to speak?"

12

John raised his hand and volunteered to share.

"I want to help people," he said. "When I grow up, I want to become a civil rights leader. I want to help others who have problems and I want to stand up for what is right. I want to make sure that all people are treated fairly." Sister Rose smiled and said, "That's Awesome, John! You've always been a really good listener and you advocate for your classmates often. I think you'll be a great activist."

"Hey Jazzi," said Sister Rose. "You're up next. What's your dream? How do you plan to use your Kuumba or Creativity to change the world?" "Um, let's see, where do I begin?" Jazzi stood up and made her grand entrance to the center of the circle as if she were taking her place on a broadway stage. "When I grow up, I think I'll become a motivator. I want to use my love for words to make the world a little greater." "Maybe someday, I'll be a teacher, a leader, or a famous MC. If I work really hard I can be anything I want to be."

14

When Jazzi went to take her seat, the entire class cheered in applause. The teacher smiled and touched her on the shoulder. The class was startled as they heard someone at the door say, "Well, excuse me." It was the Principal, Dr. Love! Everyone gasped, even Sister Rose! They thought for sure they were in for it. Instead of telling the class to use their inside voices, guess what the Principal did??? She began to rap!

15

"Yes Lil Jazzi, I think you can be, anything in life that you want, you see.
I believe that on the inside of you, is everything that you will need to make your dreams come true. When you work hard and try your best, in life you are sure to be a success!
You can be a teacher just like Sister Rose or a Rapping Principal like me, I suppose." The students nodded and cheered their principal on for the cool rhyme.

The class was dismissed and from that moment on, Little Jazzi knew just what she wanted to become when she grew up!

JAZZI'S JOURNEY : JOURNAL

When I Grow Up What Will I Be!
A Doctor, A Teacher, Maybe An MC!

_____

_____

_____

_____

_____

_____

_____

_____

_____

JAZZI'S JOURNEY : JOURNAL

When I Grow Up What Will I Be!
A Doctor, A Teacher, Maybe An MC!

_____

_____

_____

_____

_____

_____

_____

_____

_____

JAZZI'S JOURNEY :

When I Grow Up What Will I Be!
A Doctor, A Teacher, Maybe An MC!

CREATE YOUR OWN RAP

_____

_____

_____

_____

_____

_____

_____

_____

_____

_____

JAZZI'S JOURNEY :

When I Grow Up What Will I Be?
A Doctor, A Teacher, Maybe An MC!

CREATE YOUR OWN RAP

_____

_____

_____

_____

_____

_____

_____

_____

_____

JAZZI'S JOURNEY : AFFIRMATIONS

When I Grow Up What Will I Be:
A Doctor, A Teacher, Maybe An MC!

_____

_____

_____

_____

_____

_____

_____

_____

_____

_____

JAZZI'S JOURNEY : AFFIRMATIONS

When I Grow Up What Will I Be!
A Doctor, A Teacher, Maybe An MC!

_____

_____

_____

_____

_____

_____

_____

_____

_____

When I
Grow Up
What Will I Be?
A Doctor,
A Teacher,
Maybe An MC!